TEDDY BEARS

MARTIN LEMAN'S TEDDY
BEARS

PELHAM BOOKS
Stephen Greene Press

This book belongs to

PELHAM BOOKS

Published by the Penguin Group
27 Wrights Lane, London W8 5TZ. England
Viking Penguin Inc., 40 West 23rd Street, New York, New York 10010, USA
The Stephen Greene Press, 15 Muzzey Street, Lexington, Massachusetts 02173, USA
Penguin Books Australia Ltd, Ringwood, Victoria, Australia
Penguin Books Canada Ltd, 2801 John Street, Markham, Ontario, Canada L3R 1B4
Penguin Books (NZ) Ltd, 182-190 Wairau Road, Auckland 10, New Zealand

Penguin Books Ltd, Registered Offices: Harmondsworth, Middlesex, England

First published 1989

Copyright © Jill and Martin Leman 1989
Copyright © photographs Martin Leman

Research and design by Jill Leman

Typeset by Goodfellow & Egan, Cambridge
Printed and bound in Italy by L.E.G.O.

A CIP catalogue for this book is available from the British Library
Library of Congress Catalog Number 89-60796

ISBN 0 7207 1885 6

Twice Times

There were Two little Bears who lived in a Wood,
And one of them was Bad and the other was Good.
Good Bear learnt his Twice Times One –
But Bad Bear left all his buttons undone.

They lived in a Tree when the weather was hot,
And one of them was Good, and the other was Not.
Good Bear learnt his Twice Times Two –
But Bad Bear's thingummies were worn right through.

They lived in a Cave when the weather was cold,
And they Did, and they Didn't Do, what they were told.
Good Bear learnt his Twice Times Three –
But Bad Bear *never* had his hand-ker-chee.

They lived in the Wood with a Kind Old Aunt,
And one said *'Yes'm,'* and the other said *'Shan't!'*
Good Bear learnt his Twice Times Four –
But Bad Bear's knicketies were terrible tore.

And then quite suddenly (just like Us)
One got Better and the other got Wuss.
Good Bear muddled his Twice Times Three –
But Bad Bear coughed *in his hand-ker-chee!*

Good Bear muddled his Twice Times Two –
But Bad Bear's thingummies looked like new.
Good Bear muddled his Twice times one –
But Bad Bear *never* left his buttons undone.

There may be a Moral, though some say not;
I think there's a moral, though I don't know what.
But if one gets better, as the other gets wuss,
These Two Little Bears are just like Us.
For Christopher remembers up to Twice Times Ten . . .
But *I* keep forgetting where I've put my pen.*

*So I have had to write this one in pencil.

A. A. Milne

A Folk Tale

One day a bear was prowling through the forest when he came upon a fox, enjoying a meal of fish that he had stolen from the farmer.

'Hello, brother,' cried the bear. 'Where did you get that fine fish?'

The fox wiped his mouth with his paw.

'Where?' he said. 'Why, I fished for that fish in the lake, of course.'

'Can I get some too?' the bear asked.

'Surely,' said the fox. 'Just go to the lake and hang your tail down through the ice. When the fish bite at your tail, all you need to do is to jerk them out quickly from the water.'

The bear did as he was told. He dropped his long shaggy tail through a hole in the ice, and sat there waiting. He sat for a very long time until night came, but he caught no fish. By-and-by his tail froze fast into the ice.

At last the bear grew tired; he thought he would go home. When he tried to get up his tail was held fast. He pulled and he jerked and he pulled, and at last his tail snapped off short.

And that is why the bear has no tail, to this very day.

Traditional

Little Bear

B was once a little bear,
Beary,
Wary,
Hairy
Beary,
Taky cary,
Little Bear!

Edward Lear

Teddy Bear

Round and round the garden,
Like a teddy bear,
One step, two step . . .
Tickle you under there!

Anon

Archie

Safe were those evenings in the pre-war world
When firelight shone on green linoleum;
I heard the church bells hollowing out the sky,
Deep beyond deep, like never ending stars,
And turned to Archibald, my safe old bear,

Whose woollen eyes looked sad or glad at me,
Whose ample forehead I could wet with tears,
Whose half moon ears received my confidence,
Who made me laugh, who never let me down.
I used to wait for hours to see him move,
Convinced that he could breathe. One dreadful day
They hid him from me as a punishment:
Sometimes the desolation of that loss
Comes back to me and I must go upstairs
To see him in the sawdust, so to speak,
Safe and returned to his idolator.

Sir John Betjeman

Us Two

Wherever I am, there's always Pooh,
There's always Pooh and Me.
Whatever I do, he wants to do,
'Where are you going to-day?' says Pooh:
'Well, that's very odd 'cos I was too.
Let's go together,' says Pooh, says he.
'Let's go together,' says Pooh.

'What's twice eleven?' I said to Pooh,
('Twice what?' said Pooh to Me.)
'I think it ought to be twenty two.
Just what I think myself,' said Pooh.
'It wasn't an easy sum to do,
But that's what it is,' said Pooh, said he.
'That's what it is,' said Pooh.

So wherever I am, there's always Pooh,
There's always Pooh and Me.
'What would I do?' I said to Pooh,
'If it wasn't for you,' and Pooh said: 'True,
It isn't much fun for One, but Two
Can stick together,' says Pooh, says he.
'That's how it is,' says Pooh.

A. A. Milne

The Bear and the Bees

Once a bear was stung by a bee. The sting made the bear so angry that he pushed over the beehive. At once the whole swarm of bees chased him. The bear rushed indoors, but there was nowhere he could hide from the buzzing bees. 'Oh dear!' he thought. 'If only I hadn't lost my temper over one sting I wouldn't have all this trouble.'

Traditional

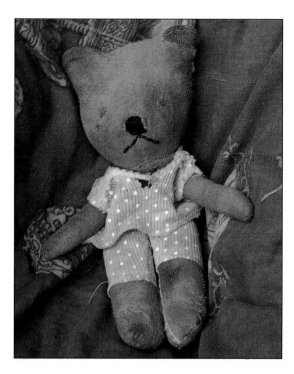

Teddy Bear

Teddy bear, teddy bear turn around.
Teddy bear, teddy bear touch the ground.
Teddy bear, teddy bear go up stairs.
Teddy bear, teddy bear say your prayers.
Teddy bear, teddy bear switch off the light.
Teddy bear, teddy bear say good night.

Skipping Rhyme

Honey Bear

There was a big bear
Who lived in a cave;
His greatest love
Was honey.
He had twopence a week
Which he never could save,
So he never had
Any money.
I bought him a money box
Red and round,
In which to put
His money.
He saved and saved
Till he got a pound,
Then he spent it all
On honey.

Elizabeth Lang

Furry Bear

If I were a bear,
    And a big bear too,
I shouldn't much care
    If it froze or snew;
I shouldn't much mind
    If it snowed or friz –
I'd be all fur-lined
    With a coat like his!

For I'd have fur boots and a brown fur wrap,
And brown fur knickers and a big fur cap.
I'd have a fur muffle-ruff to cover my jaws,
And brown fur mittens on my big brown paws.
With a big brown furry-down up to my head,
I'd sleep all the winter in a big fur bed.

A. A. Milne

Moppsikon Floppsikon

There was an old person of Ware
  Who rode on the back of a Bear,
  When they asked, 'Does it trot?' –
  He said, 'Certainly not!
He's a Moppsikon Floppsikon Bear!'

Edward Lear

Teddy Bear

A bear, however hard he tries,
Grows tubby without exercise.
Our Teddy Bear is short and fat,
Which is not to be wondered at;
He gets what exercise he can
By falling off the ottoman,
But generally seems to lack
The energy to clamber back.

Now tubbiness is just the thing
Which gets a fellow wondering;
And Teddy worried lots about
The fact that he was rather stout.
He thought: 'If only I were thin!
But how does anyone begin?'
He thought: 'It really isn't fair
To grudge me exercise and air.'

For many weeks he pressed in vain
His nose against the window-pane,
And envied those who walked about
Reducing their unwanted stout.
None of the people he could see
'Is quite' (he said) 'as fat as me!'
Then with a still more moving sigh,
'I mean' (he said) 'as fat as I!'

One day Teddy falls from the nursery window
and lands at the feet of a stout but handsome man –
Teddy recognises his hero from a picture in a book . . .

'Are you,' he said, 'by any chance
His Majesty the King of France?'
The other answered, 'I am that,'
Bowed stiffly, and removed his hat;
Then said, 'Excuse me,' with an air,
'But is it Mr Edward Bear?'
And Teddy, bending very low,
Replied politely, 'Even so!'

They stood beneath the window there,
The King and Mr Edward Bear,
And, handsome, if a trifle fat,
Talked carelessly of this and that . . .
Then said His Majesty, 'Well, well,
I must get on,' and rang the bell.
'Your bear, I think,' he smiled. 'Good-day!'
And turned, and went upon his way.

A bear, however hard he tries,
Grows tubby without exercise.
Our Teddy Bear is short and fat,
Which is not to be wondered at.
But do you think it worries him
To know that he is far from slim?
No, must the other way about –
He's proud of being short and stout.

A. A. Milne

Zoo Bear

A cheerful old bear at the zoo
Could always find something to do.
    When it bored him to go
    On a walk to and fro,
He reversed it, and walked fro and to.

Anon

Lines and Squares

Whenever I walk in a London street,
I'm ever so careful to watch my feet;
　　And I keep in the squares,
　　And the masses of bears,
Who wait at the corners all ready to eat
The sillies who tread on the lines of the street,
　　Go back to their lairs,
　　And I say to them, 'Bears,
Just look how I'm walking in all the squares!'

And the little bears growl to each other, 'He's mine,
And soon as he's silly and steps on a line.'
And some of the bigger bears try to pretend
That they came round the corner to look for a friend;
And they try to pretend that nobody cares
Whether you walk on the lines or squares.
But only the sillies believe their talk;
It's ever so portant how you walk.
And it's ever so jolly to call out, 'Bears,
Just watch me walking in all the squares!'

A. A. Milne

Grizzly Bear

If you ever, ever, ever meet a grizzly bear,
You must never, never, never ask him *where*
He is going,
Or *what* he is doing?
For if you ever, ever, dare
To stop a grizzly bear,
You will never meet *another* grizzly bear.

Mary Austin

We should like to thank the following who so kindly lent
their teddy bears for the photographs:
Deborah Ashforth, Tom & Dan Bristow, Terry Brunyee, Jenny Devereux,
Julia Dummett, Louise and Ben Foreman, Diana Green, Natalie Gibson,
Sarah Hellings, Martin Jones, Wendy Jacobs, Muriel and Edward Kenny,
Jane Moyes, Isobel Pulley, Teeny Shalev, Maureen Vanhinsberg,
Pieter van der Westhuizen, Cheryl Wells, Paul Wheeler, Marie Wylde,
Elizabeth, Henrietta and David Winthrop, Valerie Woodburn.

We should like to thank the following for permission
to use poems and extracts:
A. A. Milne, Methuen Children's Books and E. P. Dutton for poems from
'Now we are six' and *'When we were very young'*. Sir John Betjeman and
John Murray (Publishers) Ltd for the extract from *'Summoned by Bells'*.
Elizabeth Lang and Unwin Hyman Limited for *'Honey Bear'* from
'Book of 1,000 poems.'
Mary Austin and Houghton Mifflin Company for *'Grizzly Bear'* from
'The Children Sing in the Far West.'

The editor and publisher apologise for any omissions and would be pleased
to hear from those whom they were unable to trace.